Albert
the Handydog

Albert the Handydog

Stew, Shocks and Soap

Darren & Abigail Baker

Matador
9 Priory Business Park
Kibworth Beauchamp
Leicestershire LE8 0RX, UK
Tel: (+44) 116 279 2299
Fax: (+44) 116 279 2277
Email: books@troubador.co.uk
Web: www.troubador.co.uk/matador

ISBN 978 1783063 550

British Library Cataloguing in Publication Data.
A catalogue record for this book is available from the British Library.

Typeset in 15pt Book Antiqua by Troubador Publishing Ltd, Leicester, UK

Matador is an imprint of Troubador Publishing Ltd

This book is inspired by our pug dog Albert and dedicated to our beautiful daughter, Lily

Let me introduce you to my good friend, companion and all round useful chap, Albert the Handydog. He lives in this neighbourhood with the Bunting family at 23 Leaf Lane. As you can see, under his scruffy fur he has a friendly face, with a flat nose and two black panda eyes. You may have noticed the belt around his middle that has a special container for all his tools; he wears this whenever he leaves the house (and sometimes in the house) because a pug never knows when he may need his tools.

Now, if you were to come across him in the street you may be forgiven for at first mistaking him for a border terrier, or a scruffy teddy bear, or a small fluffy panda gone wrong, or even (as one family member did on a rather awkward visit to the bathroom) a toilet brush! But don't be fooled, Albert may have some image issues but don't you think for one minute this earnest little fellow does not know who he is or what he does. No. He is Albert the Handydog, here to lend you a hand, whenever you need a… well a paw really.

There is of course – as every story has – one teeny tiny problem. It's hardly worth mentioning but I feel I ought. It's just that, although Albert is always ever so keen to lend a hand, turning his paw to fix almost anything, he seems to always get things wrong. Be it a misunderstanding, a mistake or a bit of bad luck, Albert often ends up in a bit of bother.

And it is on this note our story begins…

It was a cold, windy autumn day; leaves had turned many golden colours and were falling quickly to the ground. Albert's coat was thickening with the cold and this season he was looking particularly wiry. With the hair-raising wind, it had been remarked by a number of passers by that he somewhat resembled a bottle-brush.

On this rather blustery day, Albert found himself up a particularly long ladder doing his very best to, firstly, not wobble off and, secondly, to clear the leaves from the gutter of Old Major Brandy's house. Old Major Brandy (who, incidentally, was bizarrely called so as a result of him being rather partial to a spot of whisky!) lived on his own just around the corner from the Buntings' house. He often employed Albert to help out with the odd job or two; sometimes, Albert suspected, just so he could complain about how Albert had done it. Today he had been particularly cranky. Albert had spent half the day

shifting boxes of old war memorabilia around Major Brandy's garage, in an attempt to organise the many, many, many items collected from his days as an Army Engineer Dog, and the second half wavering on the top of a very unstable ladder.

'Are you sure you're doing that right?' barked Major Brandy. 'And do be careful with where your mucky paws go. You've missed some! I'd go up there myself if it wasn't for my wonky leg. I was an Army Engineer Dog you know.

Albert rolled his eyes, but, being the patient dog he is, never complained. Nonetheless he was particularly pleased to have finally completed the task to Old Major

Brandy's satisfaction and began to head home, wanting nothing more than to have a nice hot, peaceful bubble bath.

As Albert approached the house, dreaming of scented candles, bubbles and rubber ducks, he became slowly aware that something was amiss. There seemed to be a lot of banging and, if he wasn't mistaken, Albert thought he could make out what sounded like Mrs Bunting moaning. Quickening his pace, Albert approached the front door. Reaching cautiously for the handle, he opened the door slowly. What confronted Albert then, could only be described as a wave of panic. The chaotic scene that unfurled before his eyes was like no other that Albert had experienced in his short life.

Mrs Bunting was stoanding in front of many bubbling, whistling and steaming pans. Her normally perfect hair was in a not too dissimilar style to his own; it perhaps was more of a bird's nest than a bottle brush. Albert wondered if this was now the fashion, but the beads of sweat trickling down her panicked, tomato-red face suggested that now wasn't the time to ask.

As for Mr Bunting, he was running frantically from one side of the room to

the other with the best crockery, seemingly just moving it from one place to another and back again.

'Albert, where have you been. Trust you to be out gallivanting when we needed your help!' exclaimed Mrs B.

Before Albert had a chance to answer back, Molly, the Buntings' daughter and Albert's bestest friend, appeared from under a pile of clean bed linen she was taking upstairs and said, 'Don't worry Mum, I'll sort him.'

Sort what? thought a bewildered Albert, as he was hurried to one side.

'Now listen carefully Albert, there's been a bit of news.' Albert had guessed that already. 'Mum got a phone call about an hour ago from her sister, Aunt Petunia. There was a problem with Aunt Petunia's hotel booking and so she is going to stay the night here. She has a very important business meeting in town tomorrow morning.' Now Albert had heard mention of Aunt Petunia, Mrs Bunting's very successful and rich sister, but had not met her, and from what he could pick up from the general atmosphere, that was a good thing!

'So Albert,' continued Molly, 'there is to be absolutely no shenanigans from you today. That means none of your magic tricks…'

'What's wrong with my magic tricks?' interrupted Albert.

'Let me just say three words to you, Albert. Grandma. Flour. Best dress.'

'That's four.'

Molly rolled her eyes. 'I'm serious Albert, no jelly in boots, no whoopy cushions and this is most definitely not the time for one of your songs! Mum is so stressed she is practically laying eggs and Dad can't possibly move any more plates around the kitchen before she starts throwing them at him. So quickly go and wash your paws and come and help lay the table.'

Albert did as he was told, although he was rather put out that this Aunt Petunia was causing everyone to make such a fuss and, what's more, stopping him from having his nice, hot bubble bath. But, he thought, as he returned downstairs, at least he would get one later, and if his nose detected right Mrs Bunting was making her best lamb stew for dinner. As he reached the last step and was about to enter the kitchen, the doorbell rang.

Everyone froze.

Mr Bunting broke the silence as the bowl he was carrying slipped out of his hands and fell to the floor with a loud *smash*, breaking into a thousand little pieces. Mrs Bunting gave him one of her glares as he nervously got down on his hands and knees to clear up the smashed china. Molly and Albert decided now would be a good time to retreat to the dining room and set the table. Mrs Bunting wiped her hands on her apron, made a vain attempt to straighten her hair, took a deep breath and opened the door.

Albert peered through the pug hatch to get a better look at who had arrived. Standing there were two of the strangest-looking humans he had ever set his eyes on. Aunt Petunia was the tallest, skinniest, biggest-nosed woman he had ever seen. With her *very* long neck and her long, plastic eyelashes, Albert considered she might actually be related to a giraffe rather than Mrs Bunting. Cowering behind her was a sniffling, red-headed man, waylaid with what seemed like enough luggage to move all Albert's worldly belongings ten times! Uncle Gerald, Albert presumed.

'Welcome. Come on in. Let Mr Bunting help with those bags. How was your journey?' Mrs Bunting said, through what seemed like gritted teeth.

'Terrible,' replied the pointy-nosed giraffe, as she shifted her mobile phone from her ear to kiss the air next to her sister's cheeks. 'Really sister you have let yourself go, I barely recognised you.'

'Well you're looking fabulously stylish as always,' replied Mrs Bunting.

Aunt Petunia ignored this compliment. Albert thought it was a strange thing for Mrs Bunting to say; as far as he understood from the dancing show on telly, fabulous meant good!

The giraffe wafted around the kitchen. Through the hatch Albert could see her eyes flick around disapprovingly. 'Quite amazing. This is actually the smallest kitchen I have ever been in, so quaint. Like… erm, what do you call those small people?'

'The Borrowers,' Albert piped up through the hatch.

Aunt Petunia, ignoring where this answer came from, said, 'No, it's like a gnome's house!' she laughed haughtily at her own joke. Mrs Bunting smiled awkwardly.

'Well we like it,' Mr Bunting retorted, as he struggled to carry the suitcases up the stairs followed quietly by Aunt Petunia's red-headed husband (who now had a face just as red).

'Anyway sister, don't you have a child? Where is it?'

Molly and Albert slowly made their way from the safety of the next room and entered the kitchen.

'Arghhhh! What's that?' Aunt Petunia screamed. Albert looked behind him to see what all the fuss was about.

Hurriedly Mrs Bunting introduced them. 'This is Molly, my daughter, and this is Albert the Handydog, he lives with us.'

'No, this absolutely won't do. A dog in the kitchen! It's filthy.'

Albert almost pointed out that he would have been a lot cleaner if she hadn't decided to turn up on their doorstep before he had been able to have that nice relaxing bubble bath, but sensing the mood he thought better of it.

'Molly, will you take Albert out to his kennel? Petunia do take a seat at the dining table, dinner will be served shortly.'

Molly and Albert looked at her in confusion. Not only did Mrs Bunting seem to be having a bit of a funny turn as her left eye was blinking and her head was nodding vigorously towards the door, but everybody in the household knew about the issues Albert had with his outside residence. There had been some technical difficulties with the roof and the extension was a work in progress. It was used for storage by the family at the moment, and never referred to as a "kennel". Albert was not the sort of dog to reside in a kennel, of that he was sure. He needed his creature comforts – like a lamb stew and a hot bath!

But before he knew it, Mr Bunting had returned downstairs and Albert found himself in the cold, damp kennel, with some meaty blobs in a bowl that Mr Bunting called "dog food". Whatever it was called, Albert was not eating it, it made his stomach turn.

'Don't look at me like that,' said Mr Bunting as Albert looked up at him with big sad eyes. 'You are the lucky one, out here in peace, think about us in there with her!'

Albert didn't feel lucky and it was also just his luck that the weather had now turned from blustery to rainy and the hole in the roof was letting in water

'Knew I should have fixed that first,' Albert mumbled to himself as he slumped next to the half built fancy-snack dispenser.

Having sat feeling sorry for himself for what had seemed like a very long time, Albert decided to have a look through the window into the house, just to see how things were going. He stood on his tiptoes and peered in through the window at the warm scene. The table was smartly dressed with the Buntings' best plates and glasses. His portrait (one of his most handsome ones he might add) looked down on the family sitting around the table eating steaming hot lamb stew. Albert's tummy rumbled. Through the window he could just make out Aunt Petunia's annoying voice complaining between mouthfuls and then taking incredibly important business phone calls.

Tail down (and this, for those of you who know about pugs, is a very hard thing for a pug to do), Albert returned to his "kennel" and went to sleep.

Albert woke up after what was quite a long nap – mainly because the leaking roof had now formed a puddle on the floor of the kennel – and decided he would investigate again. It was now completely dark and the lights were all off downstairs. Deciding that everyone was now in bed, Albert thought it would be a perfect opportunity to fetch the long ladder that he had used earlier that day, prop it up against the wall by the bathroom window that was usually left slightly ajar, climb in and have that long awaited bubble bath! What a brainwave!

Now what was to happen next was not in Albert's original plan, and to say who was the most shocked and upset from the whole experience would be hard for you to decide.

As he reached the top of the ladder, Albert realised that the bathroom light was left on.

Strange, Albert thought to himself, *Mr Bunting is always so vigilant about saving electricity.* He grabbed the top of the ladder with one hand and the edge of the window with his other, slowly pulling it back. He peered around.

Then came a horrible, horrible noise.

'Arrrrghhh! There's an intruder breaking into your house!' a voice screeched like a squawking parrot. 'Help! Help! Call the police!' came Aunt Petunia's shrill voice, which was shortly followed by a loud plop as her precious mobile phone slipped out of her claw-like hand, and flew through the air before nose-diving to the bottom of the sink.

How Albert didn't fall off the ladder, he would never know. The ghostly face of Aunt Petunia, the shrill scream and the wave of water all hit him within seconds and was enough to frighten even the bravest of Handydogs.

A broom entered the bathroom, shortly followed by Mrs Bunting and Mr Bunting, already on the phone to the police.

'Who is it, I'll have 'em!' Mrs Bunting squealed, waving the broom around dangerously.

As their eyes focussed, they looked first at the hair-netted, face-creamed

Petunia and then the rather pale-looking face of Albert at the window. Molly and Uncle Gerald appeared at the door. Surveying the scene and soon realising what happened, they covered their mouths, both trying to stifle a laugh.

'It's Albert, sister. Nothing to panic about, though what he's doing up a ladder at this hour I don't know,' Mrs Bunting retorted, giving Albert her glaring look.

'A dog up a ladder! I always felt you were a bit mad sister but this is going too far – this is not normal behaviour…' Aunt Petunia stopped mid-rant as her eyes fell on the sink and its sorry sunken treasure.

'My phone…!' wailed Aunt Petunia.

There was more panic. Albert, still in shock, decided now would be a good time to climb down the ladder and retreat to somewhere quiet.

Molly, seeing him silently disappear, ran down to let him into the house.

'Molly I've had a terrible fright!' trembled Albert.

'I know, so has everyone,' Molly giggled.

'But I thought it was a ghost…' said Albert, not understanding why Molly was laughing so much, but he appreciated the hug she gave him.

Amongst the commotion he could hear Mr Bunting on the phone to the local police station. 'No, no officer, there has been a misunderstanding. No one is breaking in. No need to come down,' he laughed nervously. 'What's that you say? The crying? Oh nothing, just a mobile phone. No, not stolen, just wet. Hmmm. Yes, Gerald is trying to dry it out with the hair-dryer but we will try a radiator overnight. Yes, thank you. Sorry to trouble you. Night.' As he put the phone down Mr Bunting spotted Albert's head reappear at the top of the stairs.

'Alberrrrrt!' Quicker than he could even blink, Albert found himself back outside. Molly, who was still trying to stop laughing, could see how shocked Albert looked and how cold and wet it was outside and so smuggled the car keys out to him.

'Here, best lay low tonight till things settle. Take the car keys and sleep in there.'

A very tired and relieved pug went down the driveway, pressed the unlock button on the keyring, watched the lights flash and climbed into the car. He put the key in the ignition, turned the heater on and snuggled down with his favourite book, hoping for a good night's sleep.

Albert overslept. He woke up to hear voices coming out of the house.

'If there is anything we can do to make up for the loss of your phone…' came Mrs Bunting's apologetic voice.

'No, no…' Aunt Petunia replied in her business-like voice. 'And I admit wanting to exterminate the ratty little dog of yours last night was a bit extreme. But I had had a terrible shock and suffered such a traumatic loss.'

As he came to, Albert realised that he was not curled up on the lumpy, grubby, torn seat of Mr Bunting's car, but on a very new, very plush leather seat. As he looked around at the polished interior he realised, with sheer terror, that he had not fallen asleep in the family's car but Aunt Petunia's swanky

new sports car! Albert shot up and took the keys out of the ignition. As he opened the door on the far side, so as not to be seen from the house, he could hear Mrs Bunting continue to apologise profusely about the phone.

'Anyway the bill will be in the post. And if I lose out on this very important business deal, you can forget about ever seeing me again.'

Albert smiled to himself as he quietly closed the door. *Surely that would not be a bad thing*? he thought. Molly, who had just spotted him, took the keys.

'Come along now Gerald, I've got to get there, snappy.'

Everyone's eyes fell on poor Uncle Gerald who was fumbling about in his pocket looking for the keys. 'Is this what you are looking for?' Molly handed him the key. 'You left it on the sideboard.'

Looking relieved, everyone helped Gerald load the car with all the suitcases. Goodbyes were exchanged and Uncle Gerald put the keys into the ignition and turned them ready to set off. Nothing. He tried again. Still nothing.

Aunt Petunia's face was getting redder and redder. Everyone looked flustered.

'I'll have a look,' offered Mr Bunting, as he stuck his head under the car

bonnet. 'Hmmm,' his voice became muffled, 'that's strange, your battery's flat. Like you left the lights on all night or something.' Molly turned and looked at Albert, who was skulking into the background. Albert had run the battery flat by having the heater on all night.

All the terrible news of the situation hit Albert fast. If they couldn't get it started Aunt Petunia would be even angrier and, even worse, may have to stay until the car was sorted. That may mean more nights in the kennel, with tinned dog food and no bubble bath! Albert needed to think quickly. Then suddenly an idea came to him.

Quick as a flash he ran off to Old Major Brandy's house. He was an engineer in the war. He would know what to do!

Returning to find Aunt Petunia in more tears, Albert somewhat triumphantly handed Mr Bunting Old Major Brandy's jump leads. 'Apparently you have to attach these wires from the little bits on the top of the engine in this car to the same knobbly bits on the top of the engine in your car, Mr Bunting. And then you turn your engine on and the power from your old car charges up this

swanky sports car. They are called jump leads. Though Major Brandy was unclear as to what exactly jumps.'

Major Brandy's instructions were carried out with precision. Albert watched as Mr Bunting revved his engine and electricity travelled down the wires. He waited for something to jump but the only thing he saw jump was Aunt Petunia back into her car as soon as their engine started to rev.

To everyone's relief the car was re-started. The visitors hastily drove away, hopefully, Albert thought, never to be visiting again.

A huge sense of calm ran over the family as they all turned to look at Albert.

'I can never thank you enough,' whispered Mr Bunting, as they all returned to the house.

'What can we do to repay you for saving the day Albert?'

Albert thought a minute and then replied, 'Some leftover stew and a nice, peaceful bubble bath!'